1st
Reader   991268
Reader   Gaines, Isabel
GAI   Pooh's surprise
          basket

DATE DUE

MR 28 00	MAR 2 3 2004	
	FEB 2 0 2005	
MY 18 00	JUL 3 - 2006	
JY 17 '00	MAR 15 2007	
OC 17 '00	DEC 2 7 2007	
DE 1 4 00	FEB 0 7 2008	
JE 01 01	MAR 2 6 2009	
OCT 0 1 2000	JUN 2 0 2013	
JAN 0 5 2001	JAN 2 8 2014	
JAN 2 4 2002		
MAR 1 3 2000		
SEP 0 7 2004		

1st
Reader
GAI

Pooh's Surprise Basket

Disney's
Winnie the Pooh First Readers

Disney's
A Winnie the Pooh First Reader

Pooh's Surprise Basket

Adapted by Isabel Gaines

ILLUSTRATED BY Josie Yee

DISNEY PRESS

NEW YORK

Pooh's Surprise Basket

The first of May

was a beautiful spring day.

Pooh decided to take a walk.

Pooh loved this time of year.

He sang a tune about it:

"Oh, I love spring.

Dum-dee dum-dum.

It makes me sing.

Pum-dee pum-pum.

I pick spring flowers.

Dum-dee dum-dum.

I could do that for hours!

Pum-dee pum-pum."

At home, Pooh looked

at all the flowers

he had picked.

"These flowers are so pretty,"

he said.

"I should share them

with my friends."

13

Pooh got an idea.

"I can surprise everyone

with flower baskets

made just for them."

Pooh got right to work.

Pooh started with Piglet's basket.

He gathered clover and buttercups,

the smallest flowers he had picked.

He put them in the smallest basket.

Pooh held up Piglet's basket and smiled.

"A tiny basket," he said aloud.

"Tigger's turn!" said Pooh.

Pooh tossed a bunch

of flowers in the basket.

They went every which way.

"A messy basket," said Pooh.

For Rabbit, Pooh chose flowers
of the same color.
Carefully he cut them
all to the same size.

"A neat-and-tidy basket," he said.

For Roo's basket, Pooh

went to the cupboard.

He pulled out several bouncy balls.

He put them in the basket,

and added some flowers.

"A fun basket!" he said.

Pooh made a pretty basket for Kanga,

a wise basket for Owl,

and an Eeyore basket for Eeyore.

It was full of sticks and stones.

Pooh placed the last basket

on the table.

He was ready to make

Christopher Robin's basket.

He reached for the flowers.

But there was a problem.

NO MORE FLOWERS!

"Oh dear!" cried Pooh.

"What will I put

in Christopher Robin's basket?"

"Ah-ha!" Pooh cried.

He tied a red ribbon

around the basket.

Then he gathered up

all the baskets

and ran out of the house.

Pooh left a basket at each
friend's house.
He went to Rabbit's house
and Piglet's house,
Eeyore's and Owl's.

Then he stopped by

Kanga and Roo's.

He went to Christopher Robin's

house last.

Christopher Robin was outside.

"Christopher Robin," said Pooh,

"I surprised everyone

with flower baskets.

But I wanted to give you
something extra-special." Pooh sat
down inside the basket
and said, "This is a Pooh basket.
I made it just for you!"

"Silly old bear,"

said Christopher Robin.

"You are the best surprise ever!"